To:

From:

For my family, with fond memories of the Fales family Christmases —K.G.

For my nieces, Kayley and Sophia —S.G.

Text copyright © 2016 by Kallie George * Jacket art and interior illustrations copyright © 2016 by Stephanie Graegin
All rights reserved. Published in the United States by Schwartz & Wade Books, an imprint of Random House Children's Books, a division of Penguin Random House LLC.
Schwartz & Wade Books and the colophon are trademarks of Penguin Random House LLC.
Visit us on the Web! randomhousekids.com * Educators and librarians, for a variety of teaching tools, visit us at RHTeachersLibrarians.com

Library of Congress Cataloging-in-Publication Data is available upon request.
ISBN 978-0-553-52481-9 (trade) * ISBN 978-0-553-52482-6 (glb) * ISBN 978-0-553-52483-3 (ebook)

The text of this book is set in Belen. The illustrations were rendered in pencil-and-ink washes and then assembled and colored digitally.
Book design by Rachael Cole

MANUFACTURED IN CHINA
2 4 6 8 10 9 7 5 3 1
First Edition

the Lost Gift

A CHRISTMAS STORY

written by KALLIE GEORGE * illustrated by STEPHANIE GRAEGIN

schwartz & wade books · new york

One windy Christmas Eve, four little animals huddled on top of Merry Woods Hill. They were so excited, they barely felt the cold. They were waiting for Santa to fly by on his sleigh.

"There he is!" shouted Rabbit.

"Humph," said Squirrel. "That's just a cloud."

"There he is!" Rabbit shouted again.

"Humph. That's just a . . . ," Squirrel began, but this time it really WAS Santa.

They all waved, and Santa waved back. For a moment, the stars shone brighter and the air smelled like pine and peppermint.

Then a big gust of wind hit Santa's sleigh. A present tumbled down like a shooting star, landing in the woods.

"He'll be back for it," said Rabbit confidently. The others nodded.

They waited and waited. But Santa didn't come back.

"What should we do?" worried Deer.

"Let's go find it," said Rabbit. "Santa would want us to."

"Santa would want us to go home," grumbled Squirrel.

But Bird was already off.

"Come on! Come on!" she chirped.

In a square hole in the snow, they found the present.

Rabbit dug it out.

Squirrel shook it.

Chicka-chicka-chicka, it rattled.

Deer jumped. "What *is* that?"

Bird began to peck at the paper.

"Stop," said Rabbit. "It doesn't belong to us.

Look. There's a tag."

"I can read the tag! I can!" said Bird, hopping on the gift.

"'For the New Baby at the Farm. Love, Santa.'"

The New Baby! The animals had heard of the New Baby. She'd been born in the summer, when the bees buzzed and the Farmer's strawberries were sweet.

"Now the New Baby won't get her gift," gulped Deer.

"Who cares," said Squirrel. "She's not *our* baby."

"Santa cares," said Rabbit. "Santa would want us to deliver it."

"Do I look like Santa?" groaned Squirrel.

"Maybe if we had a sleigh . . . ," said Bird.

"A sleigh!" said Rabbit. "Santa has a sleigh. Let's build one."

Squirrel groaned again.

But Bird had already begun.

When the sleigh was ready to go, the animals carefully slid the present onto it and set off. The stars lit their way.

Everything was going well until they came to a big hill. Up, up, up

Deer tugged the sleigh. Rabbit, Squirrel, and Bird pushed from behind.

Finally, they reached the top, and . . .

WHOOSH!

The sleigh sped down, down, down; then—

WHOOMP!—

it landed in a snowbank.

"Humph," grumbled Squirrel, but he helped

dig it out anyway.

The animals moved slowly now. It was long past their
bedtimes. They were hungry and tired and ready to give up.
Maybe Squirrel was right, thought Rabbit. It wasn't *their* baby.

Then Rabbit thought of Santa. Santa traveled all night long. He was probably hungry and tired too. But Santa would not give up.

Rabbit began to sing.

Dashing through the SNOW,
We ARE on ouR way
Through the Merry Woods.
Pulling ouR owN Sleigh!

Soon Bird, Deer, and even Squirrel were singing along.

At last, they reached the farmhouse.

Deer pulled the sleigh onto the porch. *Clip-clop, clip-clop* went his hooves. "Shhh!" said Squirrel. But it was too late. They heard the New Baby cry.

"Who's there?" came a man's voice.

The animals leapt off the porch and hid.

They watched the Farmer open the door, holding the crying baby.

"What's this?" said the Farmer. He looked down at the gift, but the New Baby looked out into the night.

Did she see them? The animals held their breath as the Farmer picked up the gift and read the tag. "From Santa," he said to the baby. "Let's go open it." They went back inside.

"What is it?" asked Deer.

"I can see it! I can!" said Bird. "It's a . . . it's a . . ."

"A stick," groaned Squirrel. "A lumpy old stick! A stick isn't a gift!"

Even Rabbit was disappointed.

But the New Baby grabbed the stick and shook it. *Chicka-chicka-chicka,* they heard faintly through the glass.

"Great," said Squirrel. "A *noisy* lumpy stick."

They all stared through the window at the New Baby.

And the New Baby stared back. She was smiling—right at them!
For a moment, it felt as though sunshine warmed the wintry air.

Suddenly, it didn't matter that the gift was a stick. It made the
New Baby happy. And that made the animals happy.

Snow fell softly as the animals headed home, frosting their
feathers and fur. They were too tired to talk, too hungry to sing,
but no one complained. Not even Squirrel.

Above them, the stars slipped away
and the sky lightened, welcoming
Christmas Day.

When the animals got home, they couldn't believe their eyes.

There was another gift!

"Great," groaned Squirrel. "Not again."

Bird read the tag: "'For my animal helpers. Merry Christmas. Love, Santa.'"

"It's for us!" said Deer.

"Really?" wondered Squirrel. "But how did he know?"

"Santa *always* knows," said Rabbit.